**Based on the Netflix original series
teleplay by May Chan**

hmhco.com

Designed by Melissa Martin and Sarah Boecher
The type was set in Proxima Nova.
The sound effect type was created by Melissa Martin.

ISBN: 978-1-328-49578-5 (paper over board)
ISBN: 978-1-328-49506-8 (paperback)

Manufactured in China
SCP 10 9 8 7 6 5 4 3 2 1
4500748841

# CARMEN SANDIEGO™

## THE STICKY RICE CAPER

### *A GRAPHIC NOVEL*

HOUGHTON MIFFLIN HARCOURT

BOSTON NEW YORK

# WHO IN THE WORLD IS
# CARMEN
# SANDIEGO?

**FORMERLY KNOWN AS:**

Black Sheep

**OCCUPATION:**

International super thief

**ORIGIN:**

Buenos Aires, Argentina

**LAST SEEN:**

Paris, France

I was found as a baby in Argentina and raised as an orphan on Vile Island. But I longed to set out and see the world.

I couldn't wait to train at VILE's school for thieves. I wanted to become a VILE operative, traveling the world to steal precious goods.

But I knew I had to get out after discovering what VILE really stands for: Villains' International League of Evil!

My new mission: take VILE down by stealing from them to give back to their victims.

# CARMEN'S SKILLS

Super sneak, expert fighter, gadget guru, mistress of disguise

# TOOLS FOR A THIEF

## Glider Backpack

A collapsible hang glider ready to spring open whenever Carmen needs to make a dramatic entrance or quick escape.

## Red Drone

This remote-control flying drone can send a live video feed and can even hack into security systems.

# TOOLS FOR A THIEF

Earring -- Side View

Earring -- Front View

### Comm-Link Earrings

Carmen's earrings hide an advanced two-way communications device, which she uses to stay in touch with Player through every mission.

## High-Tech Makeup

This lipstick can be used to hack into security systems.

## Grappling Hook

A hook on a rope that Carmen shoots from her wrist to reach high places.

# Player

White-hat hacker

**BACKGROUND:**

Player is a teenager from Niagara Falls, Canada. He met Carmen by hacking into her phone while she was still at VILE.

**SKILLS:**

- Learns everything about every place that Carmen goes to help guide her on capers
- Remotely deactivates security systems
- Scours the web for secret signs, coded messages, and hidden clues about VILE's next moves

# Ivy

Mechanic and tinkerer

**SKILLS:**

- Operates Carmen's gadgets, like Red Drone
- Great at fixing and making things
- Always has Carmen's back

# Zack

Driver

- Great with cars, trucks, motorcycles, speedboats -- anything that goes fast
- Knows how to make a quick getaway
- Always hungry and eats almost anything...except for fish. BLECH!

**BACKGROUND:**

Ivy and Zack are street-kid siblings from Boston, Massachusetts, USA. They met Carmen when they were robbing the same donut shop, which was owned by VILE.

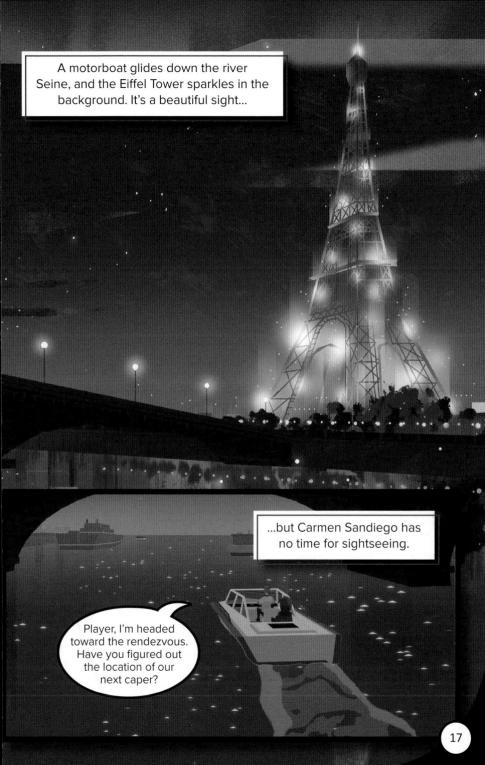

A motorboat glides down the river Seine, and the Eiffel Tower sparkles in the background. It's a beautiful sight...

...but Carmen Sandiego has no time for sightseeing.

Player, I'm headed toward the rendezvous. Have you figured out the location of our next caper?

A second boat appears on the dark river behind Carmen, with two agents that Carmen has never seen before.

Zack and Carmen race along the Seine, weaving past slower boats.

The mysterious agents are close behind.

SPLASH

Getting closer...

Up ahead, an enormous river barge makes a dangerous turn.

Three...

27

In a few seconds, the barge will block the whole channel! The two motorboats race toward a collision.

Two...

ONE!

Zack and Carmen slip past just in time...

...before the gap closes!

The barge captain appears to be confused.

SAYONARA,
MON AMIGOS!!!

Paris, France

Departure: Paris, France · Arriving: Jakarta, Indonesia

Jakarta, Indonesia

Mmm, baguettes.

Not helping, Carm!

I had my orders, little bro...

...boot the buns and cut the cheese to save your bacon.

Jakarta, Indonesia

Location: VILE Academy, Vile Island

Meanwhile at VILE Academy...

# VILE
## Academy Professors

### Gunnar Maelstrom

A psychological genius, Maelstrom learns your weaknesses and twists your mind.

### Countess Cleo

Cleo believes that ultimate wealth is ultimate power. She adores expensive everything.

## Shadowsan

A real-life modern ninja, Shadowsan teaches the criminal power of stealth and discipline.

## Dr. Saira Bellum

Death rays, invisibility fabric, brain-wiping machines -- these are Bellum's favorite things.

## Coach Brunt

Master of hand-to-hand combat, Brunt believes a butt-whooping is the solution to everything.

49

# Tigress

- Razor-sharp claws and a temper to match

- Loves bling and shiny things

- Master of quick cat-like moves and gymnastic-style stunts

- Carmen's former classmate and school rival

MRRRRRRRRMM

Carmen and her crew speed through the jungle toward the VILE hideout.

I haven't seen a single drive-thru!

I'm gonna faint from hunger here!

Just think of something other than takeout, like...stakeout.

As in, casing a joint -- you know, like the night we first met Carmen?

KRISSHHH

...and D don't stand for dollars. *Or* donuts.

Something tells me R don't stand for rubies...

And in she goes.

Red Drone's a she?

Red Drone's awesome -- of course she's a she.

Inside the lab, Red Drone spies a grid of laser beams protecting against intruders.

Red Drone weaves and bobs...

...past the deadly beams.

She connects to the lab's security system.

Your turn, Player.

CLIK
CLAK

CLIK
CLAK

Player, up for a fishing expedition?

Cosmetic and electric, Carmen's lipstick hides a jack that lets Player hack into any computer.

Casting off.

Who doesn't finish *lunch?*

Well, more rice bowls for ME.

Wait!

Zack, these aren't rice bowls.

They're *petri dishes*.

-- "super spores," to be exact: genetically engineered to *feed on rice*.

Linking feed...

I pulled the data from a folder labeled "Operation Sticky Rice."

What do you mean *feed on rice*?

These super spores take to grain like termites to wood. According to Bellum's research, these organisms can wipe out entire crops in a matter of hours.

A bioweapon.

And if VILE cleared out because they knew we were coming, they no doubt took their entire stockpile of spores with them.

Player, can you pinpoint any likely targets?

You're surrounded by likely targets: Indonesia produces 70 million tons of rice per year.

So, VILE wipes out some rice fields?

Order pizza -- problem solved, right?!

Rice is Indonesia's staple food: if crops are destroyed, its entire population could go hungry.

I like it! But how are we supposed to find teeny tiny spores in a GREAAAT BIIIIG RAINFOREST??

Hey, check it out!

...but "vile" doesn't even begin to describe how bad it was.

Just then, on a cliffside road down below, they catch sight of the truck they've been tracking.

You broke my glasses.

*You* didn't protect the face.

You may want to protect yours before I rearrange it!

UNNNGH

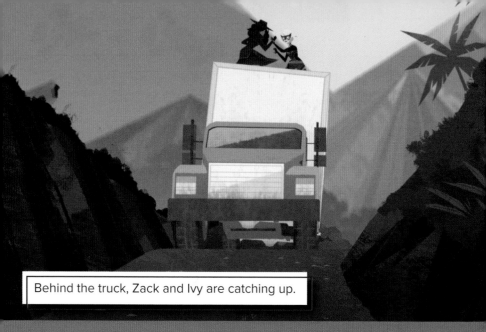

Behind the truck, Zack and Ivy are catching up.

RAAOORR

Carmen's occupied. I'll take the rear!

Ivy climbs over the windshield onto the front of the jeep.

AGH!

WHOA

What's in the truck, Tigress?!

Wouldn't you like to know!

Yes, I would. That's why I'm asking.

95

Durian fruit

Finally, some grub!

Yeah baby! Fruity goodness!

AWWWWW PEEEEYOOOOO, SMELLS LIKE A GIANT ROTTEN EGG!!!!!!!

Mmmm! But tastes good!

Almost...

...got it!

WAAAAA

# AAAAAAAAH!

SIS!!!!

HELP ME OVER HERE!

IVY, I'M GONNA SHOOT YOU A LINE!

Now, about that little nip and tuck...

IVY! Over here! Down below!

OOMPH

KSHHHHH

Inside the truck...

Skyrockets?

Carmen's grappling hook accidentally punctures a tire.

The jeep spins to a stop...

...as the truck speeds away with Tigress and the skyrockets in tow.

So we know that VILE is transporting fireworks in the back of the truck.

If Bellum's bioweapon requires a launch mechanism, that would explain it.

Bellum's super spores must be packed into the pods of the skyrockets.

Player, where would someone go to see fireworks around here?

Hmmmm...

CLIK CLAK

...it's not New Year's Eve and Indonesians don't celebrate Fourth of July, but there is a shadow puppet festival tonight -- not too far from you, just outside of Jakarta.

CLIK CLAK

Wayang shadow puppetry:
an Indonesian tradition more than a thousand years old.

The fireworks finale would most likely launch from behind the main stage.

I'll check it out. Meanwhile...

We're your eyes in the sky, Carm.

Until someone spikes a face plant.

Behind the stage, Tigress gets the skyrockets in place.

Dr. Bellum: bioweapons are locked, loaded, and ready to launch.

Tigress, you know the rules. Nothing must seem out of the ordinary. The fireworks must launch as scheduled -- when the puppet show is over, and not a moment before.

Carmen, you all--?

WHIP

WHHOOA

All yours, Carm!

Thanks. Now get to those skyrockets. And remember -- Green bad. Red good.

*Naturally.*

YAH!

Puppet show's over.

The next day...

135

# FRANCE
## DID YOU KNOW . . .

**Capital:** Paris

**Population:** Over 62 million people (in Metropolitan France alone)

**Official Language:** French

**Currency:** Euro

**Government:** Semi-presidential republic

**Climate:** Cool winters and mild summers; warmer along the Mediterranean

**Terrain:** Mostly flat plains and rolling hills in the north and west; mountainous Pyrenees and Alps regions in the south and east

**History:** Monarchy abolished multiple times, the last time in 1870 with the fall of Emperor Napoleon III; varying forms of republican government culminated in the Constitution of 1958, which established the semi-presidential republic government of today

**Flag:**

## FUN FACTS:

In the early twenty-first century, five French overseas entities—French Guiana, Guadeloupe, Martinique, Mayotte, and Reunion—became French regions.

France is one of the oldest nations in the world.

Tour de France is an annual bike race that traverses 2,235 miles (3,600 km) over three weeks—it's the most difficult and highly regarded bike race in the world. It begins in different places, but always ends in Paris.

France is known for its cheese, both the quality and the quantity of it, with more than three hundred recognized varieties.

French culture is one of the most influential in the world in areas such as art, literature, dance, music, fashion, cuisine, and film.

The motion picture was invented by two French brothers, Auguste and Louis Lumière, in 1895. France has been at the forefront of cinema ever since, and to this day holds one of the most celebrated events in movies each year, the Cannes Film Festival.

The Eiffel Tower in Paris is one of the most recognized landmarks in the world. It was built over the course of two years, from 1887 to 1889, to celebrate the World's Fair of 1889. It was even the world's tallest building until 1930, when the Chrysler Building in New York City was completed.

The Louvre Museum in Paris is the most visited art museum in the world, and has one of the world's greatest art collections. Perhaps the most famous work in its collection is the *Mona Lisa* by Leonardo da Vinci.

# INDONESIA
## DID YOU KNOW . . .

**Capital:** Jakarta

**Population:** Over 250 million people

**Official Language:** Indonesian

**Currency:** Rupiah

**Government:** Presidential republic

**Climate:** Tropical; hot, humid; more moderate in highlands

**Terrain:** Mostly coastal lowlands; larger islands have interior mountains

**History:** Ruled by the Netherlands until independence was declared in 1945

**Flag:**

## FUN FACTS:

Badminton is one of the most popular sports in Indonesia.

The world's largest Muslim population is in Indonesia.

Indonesia has more volcanoes than any other country in the world.

Most meals are based around rice. Nasi goreng is considered the national dish: fried rice mixed with other ingredients such as eggs, vegetables, seafood, or meat and a thick, sweet soy sauce.

Indonesia is home to many jungles and exotic animals, like the Komodo dragon.

In addition to Indonesian, people also speak English, Dutch, and hundreds of regional dialects.

Indonesia is one of the world's largest coffee producers and exporters. Its Kopi Luwak coffee is one of the most expensive in the world, going for up to $600 per pound!

Wayang shadow puppetry is performed using puppets behind a screen, casting their shadow for the audience on the other side. It is often performed at festivals and accompanied by gamelan music, a traditional Indonesian ensemble of mostly brass percussion instruments.

Follow Carmen to Ecuador
on her next adventure in
# The Fishy Treasure Caper